# THE PAINTED PIG

## A MEXICAN PICTURE BOOK

TEXT BY
ELIZABETH MORROW
PICTURES BY
RENÉ D'HARNONCOURT

AFTERWORD BY JAMES GRIFFITH

POSTSCRIPT BY
MARGARET EILUNED MORGAN AND
REEVE MORROW LINDBERGH

UNIVERSITY · OF · NEW · MEXICO · PRESS

ALBUQUERQUE

Library of Congress Cataloging-in-Publication Data

Morrow, Elizabeth, 1873–1955.
The painted pig: a Mexican picture book / text by Elizabeth Morrow;
pictures by René d'Harnoncourt; afterword by James Griffith; and
postscript by Margaret Eiluned Morgan and Reeve Morrow Lindbergh.
p. cm.
Summary; When the toymaker forgets to make him a piggy bank,
a young Mexican boy finds some clay and
tries to make one of his own.
ISBN 0-8263-2769-9 (cloth: alk. paper)
[1. Piggy banks—Fiction.  2. Mexico—Fiction.]
I.  D'Harnoncourt, René, 1901–1968, ill.
II. Title.
PZ7.M8455 Pa 2001
[E] —dc21
2001027692

To

CONSTANCE

who helped me buy a painted pig

in the market at *Cuernavaca*

# THE PAINTED PIG

H E WAS painted yellow, with pink roses on his back and a tiny rose-bud on his tail. He looked fat, but he was fed nothing at all. In his side was a small slit where you were supposed to put pennies, but his little mistress never had a centavo to drop into the hole; so his savings-bank stomach remained permanently empty.

His mistress was a little Indian girl who lived in Mexico between the smoking mountains and the cactus with red flowers. Her full name was Guadalupe Faustina Jovita Chimalpopoca, but everybody called her Pita, which is much shorter, prettier, and just as good. She was only ten years old but she wore a long blue scarf and a long skirt like her mother and also big gold ear-rings and a gold necklace. Her hair was parted in the middle, and the two braids at the back were tied together with a brown shoe-string.

Pita's brother was eight years old. His name was Felipe Camerino Victoriano Tlaxochimaco. If you say that correctly, it makes your whole tongue and all your teeth work. Like Pita he had another name not so long and wide. Most people called him Pedro. He wore brown sandals, no stockings, a red shirt, and long, white trousers. His coat was a blue and white blanket with a hole in the middle where he stuck his head. His hat was big as an umbrella, so he always had to put it on after the blanket; it would never have squeezed through the hole. It was made of bright yellow straw, and the brim had pictures on it worked in green and white wool.

Pedro always liked his sister's playthings better than his own. He had a toy general, made of glass, riding on a rooster. It was the third general his mother had given him, but glass generals are brittle and go to pieces easily. After the soldier was broken, Pedro never cared for the little rooster left

This is Pita

crowing without him. He had a yellow jumping-jack besides and two dogs, but they looked like reindeer and their heads were a little twisted. Pedro used to beg Pita to let him play with her painted pig.

" But you will break him," she said.

" Oh, no! I promise to be very careful."

" But you broke your general," his sister reminded him.

" Yes, but he wasn't strong."

" My pig isn't strong."

This is Pedro

" Yes, he is," cried Pedro. " A pig is always strong. And I like the rosebud on his tail. My dogs have such plain tails! "

" I'm afraid you will rub the roses off with your dirty fingers," Pita objected.

" My fingers aren't dirty."

" Why don't you play with your wiggly man? "

" I don't want my wiggly man. I want your pig."

Then after Pedro had begged and begged like this, Pita would run away from him and pretend not to see him or hear him wail. She would tease him by singing:

> " I ride on my pig,
>
> I gallop and jig,
>
> I jounce and I bounce,
>
> I prance and I dance,
>
> I leap and I creep,
>
> I jump and I stump! "

One day when they were tired of quarrelling Pita thought of going to Pancho, the toy-maker, and asking him to make Pedro a pig of his very own, with

" I ride on my pig "

roses on his back and a rosebud on his tail. Before they started out, she explained carefully to her own pig what they were doing and where they were going. He listened with his best savings-bank manner, which means that he did not talk himself at all. Pita made a great many gestures with her little brown hands and talked very loud, as you have to do when the other person does not say anything.

Pancho the toy-maker lived outside the city. He came to town with his pack of toys on his back about once a month. If you met him on the road and tried to buy a toy from him, he would never sell even the smallest ball or balloon. It did not matter how many pesos you offered him — he would not open his load until he reached the market.

Pita explained where they were going

He liked seeing all the other peddlers in the square and eating *tortillas* under his big umbrella when there were no customers. The man on one side of him sold fruit. He had little piles of oranges, prickly pears, and mangoes in front of him on the pavement, and a heap of about sixteen peanuts. On his head he balanced a brown tray filled with slices of pink watermelon.

Here are Pancho and the fruit-man

The man on the other side was a basket-maker. It was good business to sit near him, Pancho thought, for people would buy more toys when they had a basket to carry them home in.

When Pita and Pedro came along and asked for a toy pig painted yellow and decorated with roses, Pancho said solemnly, looking at his rows of horses, donkeys, deer, cows, and rabbits: " I'm sure you don't want a pig; nobody buys pigs any more. What you really want is a donkey. I have a beautiful burro from Puebla with a load of yellow marigolds on his back."

" No," said Pedro, " I want a pig like Pita's here."

" Please look at this rabbit," Pancho went on politely. " It is made of straw, and its ears wiggle. And I have beautiful straw horses; their tails wave naturally. A horse like this won't break like a clay pig."

" It is a pretty horse," said Pita, " but — "

" Perhaps you would like a lion," Pancho broke in. " It is very fierce; and see what large black eyes it has. Usually lions have yellow ones."

" But you don't understand," Pita said impatiently. " Pedro wants a pig just like mine. Haven't you one? "

" No," said Pancho, " I haven't had a pig like that since Christmas."

" Could you make one? " asked Pita.

These are the straw horses

" Yes — yes — I could make anything," said the man, " but I'm sorry you don't want the lion."

" Can you make it just like Pita's? " Pedro asked.

" Well, yes, I could," Pancho answered slowly. " But it would be very stupid to make two pigs exactly the same; don't you think so? How would you like a black pig with a wreath of red roses around his neck? "

" I think yellow is prettier," said Pedro. " Please make him yellow."

" All right," said the toy-maker; " he will cost five centavos " — and the children ran home.

But when they came to market the next week, Pancho had nothing for them. He said: " My grandmother has been sick. I could not work. She cried all day long because her teeth hurt, and we had to tie her head in a bag, but still the neighbours heard her."

" How could she eat with her head in a bag? " asked Pita anxiously. " Did you cut a hole for her mouth? "

" No," the toy-maker answered solemnly. " Air would get in, and that is the worst thing for sick people."

" I've been sick too," Pedro burst out proudly. " Once I had the fever, but I didn't cry — did I, Pita? "

" Not much," his sister answered, " except when Mother gave you the tea."

" It was nasty! " Pedro cried. " They put in mint — "

" And cabbage — "

" And rose-leaves — "

" And charcoal — "

" And ginger-root — "

" And butter."

" I must tell my grandmother," said Pancho. " We never have butter, but we could use lard."

The next week Pancho came empty-handed again.

" I lost my paint-brush," he explained to the children. " Perhaps the cat ate it. I looked everywhere and I tried to use a turkey-feather, but it broke."

The Saturday after that he said: " The clay didn't want to work. I'll have to wait for the full moon " — and the next week he had forgotten all about the pig.

" Are you sure you said a pig? " he asked. " I have a beautiful blue bird here that an old woman in the next village made. She took a gourd and dried it and rubbed it for two whole days to polish the back. Feel how smooth it is."

" I don't want to feel it," said Pedro sulkily.

" See what a long red beak it has," Pancho went on. " That's a thorn — I almost pricked my fingers, it is so sharp."

" I don't like birds," cried Pedro and he and Pita went away much disappointed.

They tried again in two weeks but the toy-maker had only jumping-jacks to show. His little booth was hung with them and they wiggled and danced in the wind.

This is the blue bird

" How about a fine black turkey? " he asked the children — " with eight big tail-feathers all — "

" I hate turkeys," Pedro cried.

" Or a blue fish with yellow — "

" I hate fish! "

" Or a ship — no extra charge for sails — "

" I hate ships — "

" Or a clown in striped trousers — "

" I ha — "

" With pig's bristles for whiskers — "

" — hate him the most of all! " cried Pedro.

" I think he looks a little like a pig really," gaily urged the toy-maker. " Won't he do? "

Pita and the jumping-jacks

But of course he would not, though the gold buttons on his tight trousers shone beautifully in the sun.

The next time Pancho had dishes and pots for sale, and after that windmills and balloons. The same thing happened over and over again until the children were tired of going to the market.

" I never want to see that old Pancho again! " cried Pedro, completely discouraged, as they walked home after the last attempt. He had bought a balloon, but he was too disappointed to play with it and sat down in the garden, ready to cry. Pita hid herself under the cactus bush and hoped that the mason mending the wall would not hear the sobs. Pedro was too big a boy to cry.

Suddenly to her surprise he ran towards her with a shout of delight. His hands were full of clay and he waved a trowel the gardener had given him.

" Pita! " he screamed, " I'm going to make my own pig! Pancho needn't think he is the only one who can do it. You sit right here, and in five minutes I'll show you something lovely."

" Are you going to make him like mine? " asked Pita.

" Bigger than yours! " he answered excitedly. " And perhaps I'll make him a policeman pig — or with a ranchero's hat — or riding a donkey."

This is the clown in striped trousers

He retired to a corner, shouting gaily once or twice: " I'm Pancho! I'm Pancho the toy-maker! " But that soon stopped and there was quiet in the patio for a long time. Pita sat loyally under the cactus waiting a summons to see the finished product. It seemed at least an hour to her before Pedro put his head round the bush and said rather slowly: " I'm not going to make a policeman, Pita; the coat looks funny, and it hides the tail."

There was quiet half an hour more, and then Pedro came out again to explain. " I don't like a ranchero hat on the pig — it hides his ears. I think I'll make just a plain pig."

" Yes, do," his sister answered. " Dressed-up animals look like dolls anyway."

Again there was quiet. Pita could hear the water running in the fountain and knew that Pedro must be wetting the clay. A little later he was slapping it between his hands and she heard him say: " Now you be good." Then he whistled a little, but finally that stopped. It was very stupid for Pita waiting like this with nothing to do. She counted the leaves on the bush above her head — and then the thorns on each leaf. She tried to pick a red blossom, but she pricked her thumb. She counted twenty-five slowly — fifty — one hundred — but still no word came from Pedro. Finally she got up on her

Pita sat loyally under the cactus

chair and looked over the wall. Pedro had his head in his hands. He was thinking very hard. A little bird was on his shoulder and the dogs were begging for a run, but he paid no attention.

" What are you doing? " Pita cried. " Isn't the clay good? "

Her brother uncovered his eyes and said dreamily: " I'm just trying to remember how long a pig's nose is. It's funny how I have forgotten."

" Pigs don't have noses! " Pita cried. " They have snouts, and they are quite long." Then she ran off to fetch her own pig as an example, but Pedro would not let her come near the fountain, where he had a strange pile of sand, sticks, and mud.

He worked all the afternoon, grunting like a little pig himself as he slapped and pounded the clay, added sand and water, and spread it out on a board. To all Pita's questions he answered impatiently: " Just wait — just wait a minute." She begged to help, and Pedro promised that when he came to painting the back, she might put on a stroke of yellow. It was six o'clock and the sun was reddening the white volcanoes when he finally called to her that he was done. She came round the cactus bush and looked at Pedro's pig.

" Oh, Pedro! " she cried. " Is that — is that *it?* "

Pedro was thinking very hard

" Yes," he answered slowly. " I made seven others, but this was the only one where the tail stuck."

" Isn't it rather thick? " asked Pita.

" But it won't stay on unless you make it thick," her brother answered. " And I wanted to have a curl in the tail. Don't you see the curl? "

" Yes," she said. " Aren't the ears awfully big? "

" Perhaps — but don't pigs always have big ears? "

" No — no, — Pedro — it's elephants you're thinking of."

" And his snout, Pita — it was hard to get that pointed. Do you think that's all right? "

" Well — yes — for a very big pig — a mother pig," she answered slowly " It's awfully long."

" You said snouts were always long! "

" But not *so* long."

" And his legs," Pedro continued anxiously — " I tried and tried, but I couldn't get them all alike."

" They do wobble a little," she murmured.

" Isn't *any* of him right? " asked the little artist.

Pita looked at Pedro's pig

" Oh, yes," Pita hurried to assure him. " He has a good back. I think anybody would know you meant the smooth part for his back."

" Really? " asked her brother, encouraged. " And if I could just **make** over the tail and the legs — but I'm so tired! And the clay won't work. I should have waited for the full moon. You can't make a good pig without the moon, Pancho said."

" Yes, Pedro, that must be it," his sister assented eagerly. " It's not your fault this isn't a — a — well, very piggy pig. Make another when the moon is full."

" But what shall I do with this one? " asked Pedro sadly, looking down at his handiwork.

" Let's bury him," said Pita, and they dug a hole with the trowel and laid him under the cactus. The grass soon grew over his grave, and everybody forgot him.

In the bright spring months that followed, the talk was all of kites, and Pedro and Pita had a troop of them flying over the garden. One morning they were running down the plaza to buy twine to float an unusually large red dragon when Pancho came out of his booth, smiling, with a savings-bank pig in his hand.

" I made him last night," Pancho said. " He's a grand pig, fat and strong, and he only costs five centavos."

He was painted yellow, with blue circles on his back and a large blue dot behind each ear.

" It would have been stupid to make two pigs alike," Pancho went on. " And blue looks very well on a yellow pig."

" He is wonderful! " cried Pedro, snatching him from Pancho's hand to run practised fingers over the head. " The ears aren't too big, and the nose isn't too long, and the legs don't wobble."

" They could walk to Vera Cruz," the toy-maker put in proudly.

" And he's yellow like your pig, Pita," Pedro finished. " And blue rings are just as pretty as pink roses, aren't they? "

" Almost," answered Pita, with her hand on the rosebud tail.

Then Pita picked up her skirt, and Pedro flung his blanket over his shoulder, and together they danced for joy with Pancho and the two pigs looking on.

Pita and Pedro danced for joy

# A Historically Important Pig

## BY JAMES GRIFFITH

There's a painted pig on the bookcase behind me as I write this. Not The Painted Pig, of course, but a painted pig nevertheless. It came to me shortly after my parents had visited Elizabeth Morrow in Cuernavaca, Mexico, in the mid-1930s, so I suspect she had a hand in selecting it. It contains a penny which was put in it by her famous son-in-law, Colonel Charles Lindbergh. The pig has faded over the more than sixty years of its life, and its colors are no longer as wonderful as those in this book. But it is surely a cousin to the better known Pig of Mrs. Morrow's story.

I say "better known," and I might also have said "historically important." For Elizabeth Morrow's pig stands at an important time of change in the ways in which people of the United States perceived Mexico and Mexican culture. Let me explain.

In the late summer of 1927, Dwight Morrow, a partner in the firm of J. P. Morgan, accepted an appointment from President Calvin Coolidge as United States Ambassador to Mexico. He was to prove an astonishingly wise choice for the position. While most of his predecessors had treated the Mexicans with condescension and even contempt, Ambassador Morrow actually liked Mexico and Mexicans, and went out of his way to demonstrate that liking. At a time when high-level diplomats lived at a considerable remove from all save the most socially and politically influential members of their host countries, Ambassador and Mrs. Morrow broke that pattern by taking an active and enthusiastic interest in almost all aspects of Mexican culture. Mexican music and dance were featured at official Embassy functions, the Morrows learned Spanish and showed great interest in Mexican art, and the family even purchased and remodeled a house in Cuernavaca ("Casa Mañana") and filled it with Mexican folk and fine art.

Attitudes toward Mexico and Mexican culture were changing during the 1920s and 1930s. There is a probably apocryphal account of a pre-1920 headline in *The New York Times* which trumpeted PEACE BREAKS OUT IN MEXICO. This says much about contemporary North American perceptions of Mexico as a land of revolutionary chaos. Before the revolution it had been a source of investment opportunities ensured by abundant cheap labor and a strong man–don Porfirio Díaz–at the helm. If the Indians and common folk were perceived as having culture, it was of a backwards sort. Within Mexico itself, appreciation of home-grown culture was at a low ebb as well. "Decent" people looked to France and England as civilized places, and took pride in their degree of European-ness. For them, Mexico had little or nothing to offer.

All this was changed by the Revolution. Within Mexico, artists like Roberto Montenegro, Miguel Covarrubias, and Diego Rivera discovered the folk and indigenous arts of their country and used them in their paintings and murals. Gerardo Murillo, better known as "Dr. Atl," organized the first-ever exhibition of Mexican folk art in Mexico City and Los Angeles, an exhibition that opened in 1921. It was against this background of increasing awareness of Mexican aesthetic traditions within Mexico that the work of the Morrows and their circle of friends must be seen.

Some of Mrs. Morrow's earliest entries in her diary of the Mexican years involve the enthusiastic discovery of Mexican art and antiques. Three days after her arrival in Mexico City, for instance, she bought textiles, pulque glasses, and an old wooden chest. In her first month in Mexico, this Ohio Presbyterian woman visited the Day of the Dead crafts stalls in the Alameda and was obviously fascinated by them.

The Morrows soon acquired a circle of friends beyond the diplomatic world of the capital. These included the artists Diego Rivera and Miguel Covarrubias, the American dealer and designer William Spratling, who revived the silver industry of the old mining town of Taxco, and René d'Harnoncourt, a young Austrian nobleman who collected and dealt in Mexican folk art. All of these men, with encouragement and assistance from the Morrows, went on to national and even international fame. René d'Harnoncourt served as director of the Museum of Modern Art from 1949 to 1968, after organizing landmark exhibitions of Mexican and American Indian art.

Mexico in the mid-1920s was beginning to stabilize after more than fifteen years of revolution and civil war. Problems still remained, most particularly a serious disagreement between the Socialist state and the Catholic church, which in turn led to armed conflict over much of the country. Ambassador Morrow had a strong hand in helping resolve this tragic situation; he told his wife that it was the most important thing he had done or ever would do.

At the same time Mexico was beginning once more to attract American tourists, including members of prominent East Coast families who knew the Morrows. For these people Mrs. Morrow proved a wonderful guide and hostess, taking them to shops and markets and setting an example with her enthusiastic acceptance of Mexican art and culture as well as her unerring sense of style. The late Nelson Rockefeller is said to have remarked that his interest in Mexican folk art began when as a young boy he accompanied his mother and a friend of hers on a visit to Mrs. Morrow, a visit which involved visits to village markets. Over in Taxco, William Spratling is said to have encouraged hesitant American ladies to purchase his silver by wondering out loud whether the pieces they were considering might not have been set aside for Mrs. Morrow.

Elizabeth Morrow's ties with Mexico lasted long after her husband's death in 1931. She maintained Casa Mañana for the rest of her life, inviting friends, children, and grandchildren to visit her, thus introducing a widening circle to Mexico and Mexican culture. Among her guests were my own parents. As a result of their visits to Mrs. Morrow, I grew up in an environment that was unusually accepting–for the 1940s in California—of Mexican art, food, and music. My life as a student of Mexican folklore thus has roots that go back to Casa Mañana.

The Morrows' weekend retreat in Cuernavaca got them more closely acquainted with d'Harnoncourt, who helped with the renovation, furnishing, and decoration of that showcase of Mexican tradition. He had been collecting Mexican toys for some time, and combining them in wonderful paintings with a strong sense of color. In fact, he had considered writing a children's book based on this series of pictures. Mrs. Morrow, who was already a published poet, was asked by a prospective publisher to write a story to go along with the illustrations. On September 4, 1929, she noted in her diary "I am to write the story. I want to do it!" That same month she started to write, bringing to the task her love of Mexico, its arts, people, and markets. The book was first published in 1930, and went into thirteen printings, the last in 1960.

So it was that, thanks in great part to the support and enthusiasm of the Morrows and their friends, Mexican folk art began to leave the category of "curios" and enter that of "art" for an increasing number of cultural and aesthetic trend-setters in the northeastern United States. D'Harnoncourt organized a Mexican art exhibition at the Metropolitan Museum of Art in 1930–32 under the sponsorship of the American Federation of Artists. All this helped pave the way for the milestone 1940 exhibition of Mexican art in the Museum of Modern Art, and for all that was to follow. And at an important point in this path of increasing understanding and appreciation frolics *The Painted Pig,* bringing its message to both children and adults. I just looked over my shoulder at my own pig. I think it winked at me. ◆

# Elizabeth Morrow's Mexico

BY MARGARET EILUNED MORGAN

AND REEVE MORROW LINDBERGH

IT IS A GREAT PLEASURE to know that our grandmother Elizabeth Morrow's book *The Painted Pig* will reach a new generation of readers. It is a piece of our childhood, a piece of our hearts, and also a piece of the life of a very remarkable person.

It was not unexpected that her husband, Dwight Morrow, would receive a governmental appointment from President Coolidge. What was a shock was that Coolidge appointed him ambassador to Mexico. Calvin Coolidge and Dwight Morrow had been friends since college, and Coolidge knew that if Dwight Morrow were asked to serve his country, he would want to make a genuine contribution. It is hard for us today to realize how strained relations were between Mexico and the United States in 1927. Coolidge's instructions to our grandfather were simple, to the point, and deadly serious: "My only instructions are to keep us out of war." Coolidge was never a man to exaggerate. War between the countries was a very real possibility.

Like most women who find their world turned suddenly upside down by an abrupt, unexpected change in their husband's professional life, our grandmother was in turn outraged, resigned, and, no doubt, privately dismayed. It did not help that once the appointment was made public, friends rushed to declare the appointment a guaranteed failure and therefore professional suicide for her husband, Dwight. Shortly after crossing the border, their youngest daughter Constance's West Highland White terrier escaped, pointed his nose north, and determinedly dashed toward the United States. After a dramatic rescue by car, the dog was returned. One of Dwight Morrow's associates traveling with them remarked that the dog was the only member of the party that showed any sense. It is not surprising that when Elizabeth Morrow published a collection of her poetry

in 1931 it contained a poem defending Lot's wife.

That her husband's appointment would be considered an unqualified success and one of the triumphs of the Coolidge presidency; that her future son-in-law Charles A. Lindbergh's pioneering nonstop flight between Washington, D.C., and Mexico City would diminish the profound sense of distance between the two countries; that she would come to know and love Mexican culture, and further become an ardent, respected collector of Mexican Art—that was all in the future. Had you told her at that moment that she would build a much-loved house in Cuernavaca, returning year after year for the rest of her life, she probably would have noted in her diary that night that your fortune teller was cheating you worse than usual.

Ambassador Morrow, swept into the demands of his job and affairs of state, found his place in the new country almost immediately. As is often the case, it was a subtler journey for his wife to find a role and circle of friends that suited her. Despite a hectic official schedule that she managed brilliantly, and the nagging frustrations of trying to create a sense of home in an official residence, she continued to write poetry and get it accepted in American periodicals. She also did find a remarkable circle of friends, and through the hospitality of Sir Esmond Ovey, the British Minister, and their friendship with Frederick Davis, she would be introduced to the small town of Cuernavaca.

"We [Dwight and Elizabeth Morrow and their daughter Constance] first went to Cuernavaca over the old road of cobbles and ruts that joggled slowly through the Indian villages. . . , and left one shaken in teeth and temper at the end of a three hours trip." It was not only the cobblestones that made the car trip a challenge. One shared the road with all the vibrant diversity and ingenuity of Mexican life on the move: religious pilgrims; craftsmen and farmers carrying their wares and produce to market on their backs; families with their possessions and animals. But that was not all. In the late 1920s bandits were at times a very real worry. Moreover, car radiators overheated crossing the mountains. This was a predictable enough phenomenon that when it occurred little boys would appear "as if by magic" offering cans of water at inflated prices to travelers who had not thought to bring extra water with them.

Our grandparents fell in love with Cuernavaca within hours of arrival, and once they acquired their own house, Elizabeth Morrow would be drawn into not only the frustrating but also the enchanting aspects of daily life in a country not her own. The children who lived across the way fascinated her. She learned their names and followed their games. She was also drawn to the market that, as she wrote, "was a story by itself." The ultimate charm of their house with its blend of old and contemporary Mexican art was in a great part due to the eye and flair of "our friend, Count René d'Harnoncourt." She recognized his talent as an artist and commissioned him to do a fresco for her garden. To work together on a children's book was a natural extension of their collaboration and friendship.

While we know from her diaries and other writings that she incorporated material into the book from her actual experiences—the recipe for a folk medicine and the unique logic of the character Pancho "the Toy Maker," for example—she did not overload the text with Spanish terms such as *rebozo, sombrero, sarape* or *piñata,* although she certainly knew them. Occasionally when there is no familiar American equivalent toy she will call a *piñata* or devil a jumping jack or clown. This is a deliberate attempt to make the book accessible to American readers and not a case of ignorance.

Although the promotional material for the first edition suggests that Elizabeth Morrow based her story on the children who lived across the street in Cuernavaca, the illustrations are almost entirely based on René d'Harnoncourt's extensive collection of Mexican toys. The children across the street, our grandmother sadly noted elsewhere, had no toys "except an old ball and bead strings known locally as 'tears of Job.'" D'Harnoncourt's joyful, lovingly detailed illustrations, deftly combine objects and traditions from different areas of Mexico in a manner that could cause a purist to worry if they are "authentic."

That is not really their role in a children's book that is a good part fantasy. Their role is to reflect the emotions of the characters, and to delight, frighten, and beguile their intended American audience of young readers who may or may not be reading yet for themselves.

The pictures work in an amazing number of strands of Mexican life: clothes, furniture, decorations for religious processions, religious pictures, embroidery, different craft techniques, and possibly some of the political tensions of the time. Why, in the picture of the straw horses, is Pita kneeling as if by a roadside watching the horses pass by, suddenly life size? Why is the background suddenly and uniquely black? Especially powerful is the image of the Clown with Striped Trousers, recognizable as an effigy of Judas dressed as a wealthy "hacendado" or ranch owner. Such effigies were then strong political statements carefully worked into a religious tradition. When Pedro states, "I hate him most of all," and the toy maker replies, "I think he looks a little like a pig really" is more being said? It is impossible to know, but the slightly darker side to these two plates is one of the reasons that the book, although couched in the language and customs of children's literature of its time, does not stray irretrievably into the sentimental or the saccharine.

*The Painted Pig* was an immediate success, and the first printing sold out quickly. Our grandmother would go on to write five more children's books—a second book with René d'Harnoncourt and then four more by herself. *The Pint of Judgment* would go through six printings, but none of Elizabeth Morrow's books would have as enduring a success as *The Painted Pig,* which would stay in print for thirty years. There is no question that it was a very special book for her, and when she signed a copy for her youngest granddaughter, she wrote that she hoped that they would be able to go to the market in Cuernavaca to buy a painted pig together. To the very end she wanted the book to be a door to the country and culture she had come to love. ◆